SHORT AND STEAMY DUET

TONI DENISE

✻ Created with Vellum

THE WEDDING DATE

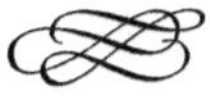

CHAPTER 1

"You can't be serious right now." Hannah plopped down on Grace's bed.

"I'm sorry, but I just can't go this weekend."

"And you can't tell me why?" None of this made any sense to Hannah. "You know I know you just don't want to go now."

"I promise, that's not it, I just had something come up."

"You were supposed to be my plus one and now you are bailing on me and being shady about it." Hannah stood up and headed to the door. "I'm just not going to go, it's so not worth it anymore."

"You can't not go, you're in the wedding party." Grace rose and followed her out the door.

Hannah threw a look at Grace. "Maybe I'll just tell her something came up."

"Please don't be mad at me. I'll tell you all about it when I can." Grace told her as they reached the kitchen.

"Not good enough, I thought I was your best friend." Hannah knew she was pouting but was helpless to stop it. *What am I supposed to do now?*

"Just go, have a good time there and hopefully I will be able to explain it to you when you get back." Grace pleaded.

"No, I can't. Greg is the best man, it was bad enough I didn't have a date, but to go alone? I don't have it in me."

"Yes, you do."

"No really, I can't show up there alone completely. I'll have no one to talk to."

"You're in the wedding party, you'll have people to talk to." Grace sounded like she was getting as frustrated as Hannah felt.

"Sorry, I'm not mad at you, I'm just confused." Hannah sat down at the bar and played with the label on her water bottle.

"I can't do this any other time, or I would. I need you to understand."

Hannah nodded, but she didn't understand. Confusion, betrayal, alone, were just a few of the emotions swirling through her head right now but she was too caught up in all of them to fight with Grace anymore for now. Instead she thought about how to get out of the wedding, maybe the stomach flu? It was a little early in the fall for that to be going around though.

She had been looking forward to going. A destination wedding, in the fall, in Vermont, was exciting, and she had been eager to get up there and show Greg she was over him too. Greg's dumping her nearly a year ago had taken its toll on her.

Just two months before their own wedding, Greg had invited her out to dinner at the same restaurant he had proposed at. She thought they were just celebrating his new job, but Greg had other plans. "I've been seeing someone else." That's how he broke it off. Over a bottle of wine and before she could leave, the ever-practical Greg wanted to discuss the financial burden of the wedding and expected her to pay for half of everything they owed on it.

She was a sucker though and agreed just to get out of the restaurant and had headed straight to Grace's and drowned her feelings in a few bottles of wine before coming back up again. It had taken months to get everything sorted and explain to everyone that there was no wedding. Meanwhile Greg had gone on about with life with Nancy and wouldn't even return her calls about the payments due.

"Hannah are you listening?" Grace interrupted her thoughts.

"No, sorry. I was thinking."

"About Greg probably," Grace mumbled. "I said I have a solution."

"What's that? A fake date?" Hannah rolled her eyes and focused back on her label.

"Actually, yeah."

Hannah whipped her head to grace so quick she nearly fell off the bar stool. "That's insane. You're insane. I'll figure something out."

"No, listen. Take Josh. Greg never met him and doesn't know he's my brother. It's perfect, he already knows you. Way better than an escort service."

"What? Who said anything about an escort service? I swear sometimes I wonder about you."

"Escort services huh?" Josh said as he walked into the kitchen, barefoot in jeans and a plain white t-shirt. The same way he was always dressed and yet, never failed to catch her interest. His sandy blond hair was on the verge of needing a cut as it starting to get that messy look after he'd run his hands through it during the day.

Hannah felt her face heat, it was just what she needed right now for Josh to walk in. She'd had the hots for them since they were kids and he'd barely paid any attention to her. Of course, she was his kid sister's friend, and he was definitely off limits. Not to mention how humiliating this was to have him standing there and Grace explaining her romantic failures to him. *I can't even get my own date, ugh.*

"What are you doing this weekend Josh?" Grace asked.

"Just hanging out since you two will be gone and I'll finally have the apartment to myself." Josh opened the fridge and pulled out a string cheese.

"About that, I'm not able to go."

"Why? You've been planning this for a while.

"She won't even tell me why," Hannah added.

"What the heck Gracie?" Josh leaned his tall frame back against the counter, and stared at her waiting for an answer.

"I can't say."

It took Josh a minute to respond as he processed her answer, or lack of one. "That's a pretty crap thing to do leaving Hannah in the lurch."

"I know, but I am going to make it better." Josh raised one brown eyebrow at Grace. "You can take her, that way Greg will think she has a date which is even better than me going." Grace sat up taller and smiled as though she had solved everything.

"Really, she's delusional, it's fine Josh. Sorry she dragged you into my mess," she threw a side glance to Grace. "A mess that she created I might add."

"Stop, it's a great solution and Josh has no plans." Grace clapped her hands together still looking pleased with herself.

For his part Josh just stood there dumbfounded watching them. He hadn't even ate his cheese from before. However, his gaze drifted to focus directly at Hannah and lingered there long enough to make her even more uncomfortable.

"Hannah," Josh begean and she prepared herself for the letdown, "This is the guy from last year? The one you were going to marry?"

Hannah nodded. "It's really not that big of a deal though. I can handle him and his new fiancé." *I hope.*

Josh continued to stare at her. It was as though he was assessing her and debating it she really could handle it. "All right, I'm in. When do we leave?"

Still prepared for a letdown, Hannah choked on her water at his words, sputtering as she coughed out the water. "What?"

"I'm in, let me know what I need to bring and when we leave. I'm driving though, I hate being the passenger."

Hannah's jaw dropped as she watched him walk away. She was dreaming, had to be, nothing else made sense. "Ouch." She rubbed her arm. "What did you pinch me for?"

"To prove this is real. You have a date to the wedding." Grace laughed.

"But, what just happened? Why did he even agree?" This had been the most confusing day of her life.

"He's a good person. He will always help when he can. Plus, he's known you forever and watched you go through that breakup so I knew he would help."

"You're insane. Both of you are. I'm going home."

"I'll let him know what to pack and tell him to pick you up at ten."

Hannah didn't even acknowledge her. There was no way he was going to show up because this didn't just happen. Not that she didn't want to bring him to the wedding and show him off to Greg, but she didn't want a pity date either. Rather than sit at their apartment She grabbed a cab and headed home to finish packing, just in case this wasn't a hallucination and she was heading to the wedding with Josh tomorrow.

CHAPTER 2

*J*osh felt bad for Hannah, that's what he told himself as he headed out the next morning to pick her up. If he was honest with himself, the reason he had spent the night packing and pacing had little to do with feeling bad for her.

Hannah had been a constant in his and Grace's life for as long as he could remember. Even when she was away at college, she video chatted with Grace so often that it was like she never left. And somewhere between her high school graduation and coming home from college, she had changed, or more like he had started to notice her.

She came home from college different, slightly more confident but still a little awkward. She went from jeans and t-shirts to professional skirts and blouses. Simply put, she had bloomed, and he had missed the transformation part. Her long auburn hair was pulled back into a ponytail everyday when they were younger, now she kept it a little shorter and usually wore it down, and he wanted to run his hands through it constantly.

That had been three years ago and even though she practically lived at their apartment, he'd done a pretty good job at pretending to be not interested. There had been a few moments where he could have stolen a kiss and he knew she would have let him, but instead he had held off. She had always been Grace's friend, and he didn't want to ruin anything. Grace had a hard time making friends when they were younger so having one that had lasted meant a lot to her.

He put his suitcase in the trunk of his car and pulled out of the parking garage. Grace had double-checked that he had packed everything, twice, but still wouldn't budge about why she wasn't going. Finally, she had asked him why he had agreed to go with Hannah so easily, and they had agreed to stop questioning each other. He'd ask Hannah if she had gotten anything out of Grace when he picked her up.

Traffic was a pain getting to Hannah's and he couldn't wait to pick her up and head out of the city. He almost never drove his own car anymore, too impatient to deal with the other drivers. It was much easier to hail a cab than to deal with his own, much less everyone else's, road rage.

He texted Hannah at the next stop light and let her know he was close. She hadn't responded but when he pulled up in front of her building, she was standing there with her suitcases, the pile of them nearly as tall as her short frame. After waiting for one car to move he quickly pulled to the side and popped the trunk. Hannah was there and putting her suitcase in before he had time to help her, leaving him feeling a little put out by not getting to be the gentleman.

"Hey thanks for coming." Hannah said as Josh closed the trunk.

"No problem. You ready?"

"I think so." She gave the shy little smile that she often used for him.

"Let's get out-of-town then. You can put the address in the GPS when we get in."

She smiled again and headed to her side of the car. Josh nearly tripped over his own feet, but he managed to get there in time to at least hold the door open. She kept her head down the whole time, but he thought he heard her mumble "thanks" before he shut the door. If she wasn't planning to look at him and to only barely talk to him, it would be a long weekend.

When they were about an hour from the resort, he couldn't take it anymore. The whole ride Hannah had spent staring out the window and giving the bare minimum response to his questions. He'd even put on a band he knew she hated and still nothing from her.

"Hannah, if we're going to pretend date, you're going to have to talk to me, maybe look at me some and pretend you like me."

Shocked, Hannah's head spun in his direction, her eyes wide. "I'm sorry, I just don't know what to expect."

"From me or your friends?"

"Both?"

"I can't answer for your friends, but for me, I am here to be the lucky boyfriend, maybe even the fiancé, and make Greg wish he had never cheated."

"I don't want to make you uncomfortable either though."

"Please stop. I wouldn't be here if I didn't want to. I can think of worse ways to spend one weekend than impressing your friends while you hang on my every word."

Finally, he got a real reaction out of her when a bubble of laughter spilled over. "Thank you for doing this." Hannah said and reached over to set her hand on his for just a moment. As she pulled her hand away, Josh quickly grabbed it and held it. She didn't pull away but sent him a confused look.

"You're going to have to touch me. We can practice now." She didn't respond, but she didn't pull away and he could feel her trying to relax. "It will be okay."

CHAPTER 3

The last leg of the trip had been both exciting and unbearable. Josh held her hand until they had gotten off the highway and then he needed to focus more on all the turns. Never in her life had she worried so much about if her palms were sweaty.

She was terrified about getting through this weekend and again contemplated bailing on everyone. She wanted to show off to Greg and everyone else, but she still wasn't prepared to pretend a relationship with Josh to do it. Oh, it wouldn't be hard to do, just hard to remember it was an act. She took another deep breath as they pulled into the drive for the resort where the wedding was being hosted.

Pulling her hand away, she set it in her own lap, ready to get out of the car. The closer they got to the front, the quicker her heart was beating. It would be a long weekend and it hadn't even really started yet.

"We're here." Josh said as he put the car in park.

She reached for the handle before Josh stopped her.

"Don't. Let me open it for you."

Without giving her time to reply, he quickly got out and walked around to her side to open the door.

"My lady." Josh made an exaggerated bow before extending his hand to help her out of the car.

She took it and stood, deciding to play along. "Thank you, good sir." She curtsied, and they both laughed. A high-pitched trio of squeals interrupted their happy moment.

"Oh. My. God. You made it!" Three women shuffled forward to greet her and pulled her away from Josh. "Did you call a service to drive you all the way up here? You know I would have sent someone!" Three pairs of eyes were staring at her in pity within a minute of getting there. *I should have stayed home.*

"That's a nice offer, but actually this is my girlfriend." Josh draped one long arm around her and pulled her in to his side.

"You didn't tell us!" Sara squealed and stepped back to take in the couple. "You guys are so cute together, aren't they girls?"

"Absolutely," The blonde, Britany, chimed in.

Allison just smiled and stared at Josh. He looked uncomfortable under the scrutiny which made Hannah confused. Was it because he was worried about cheating on their fake relationship? She hoped not because they needed to set down some ground rules.

"I did tell you I had a plus one." Hannah looked at Sara.

"Well, yes, but then you and Greg…" Not sure what to say, Sara let that sentence hang.

"Are no longer a thing. Lucky me." Josh turned to face Hannah, cupping her chin and tilting her mouth up for a kiss.

Not just any kiss either, a full-on, show-stopping, knees weakening, tongue-using kiss. It was a good thing he had ahold of her too because otherwise she would have fallen right to the ground and drowned in a puddle of embarrassment and excitement. A not-so-subtle cough had Josh stepping back and Hannah almost fell forward on to him.

With a grin and a wink he helped her straighten back up before she turned to face her friends. "Sorry about that, we're a little happy to be here."

"I can see that." Britany said eyeing her up and down.

"Come on, the valet will take the car and they'll get the bags to your room, it's mingle time!" Sara's voice got louder as she spoke until the last bit was a full-on yell.

Josh kept his arm around her shoulder and together they followed everyone into the resort. Where the outside was supposed to look rustic but was clearly designed that way, the inside was far better. Everything was stained wood as far as the eye could see. Chairs were either carved or made out of wood pieces and a giant log stood as a pillar in the center of the room. It was gorgeous and both Josh and Hannah stopped to take a look around before chasing after their host.

"Hannah, you made it." Someone reached out and touched her arm as they walked out on to the patio in search of Sara.

"Paul!" Hannah let go of Josh to give Paul a warm hug. "Josh this is Paul, the groom."

The two men exchanged greetings. Paul was the exact opposite of his bride to be, Sara. Paul was tall, dark hair, and a grin that was kept quiet except for true moments of joy. Sara was on the shorter side although always in heels, blonde, and used her stunning smile on any and everybody. Where Sara was high strung and outgoing, Paul was quiet, much more reserved. A lot like the resort they were in now.

"Paul, how in the world did you get Sara to have the wedding here?" She couldn't help it, it was all she was going to think of now if she didn't ask.

"Funny story, she gave me a list of things she wanted for

the wedding and I didn't mind the majority, so I asked to be able to overrule her on one thing no argument. She went for it and, well, here we are. Paul opened his arms and spread them out, gesturing to the place as a whole.

"That's the best. Did she still fight some?"

Paul's only answer was a wink before someone else greeted him and he turned away from Hannah and Josh. Josh took Hannah's hand and led her further out on the patio towards the refreshments.

"I should have guessed you'd be heading for the food." Hannah laughed as he grabbed a plate and started filling it up at the small buffet that was set up.

"Nope, WE were heading for the food. Grab something, you know you want to."

Hannah hesitated, but went for it anyway and grabbed a few things to put on her plate. Josh took one look at it and added to it. She shook her head but let him and then they sat at a table near the rail, overlooking the grounds, with a great view of the mountains.

"It really is amazing here." Josh said between bites.

"Right? As if the whole landscape was waiting for the perfect picture." Hannah stared out beyond the green grass and into the blue mountains beyond them while she ate. Totally engrossed, it wasn't until Josh nudged her foot with his that she realized she'd forgotten him. "Sorry."

"It's okay, really. It's amazing to look at. I'm still hungry though and wanted to know if you wanted anything else?"

Hannah smiled and shook her head, watching Josh as he headed back for the buffet and helped himself to a new plate. It was dinner time now, and this was likely all their hosts were offering for day one of the festivities as people would be arriving all day. Tomorrow was the rehearsal and the dinner to follow, then the wedding on Sunday.

"Not surprised you're sitting here alone," came the unwelcome voice from behind her.

Chills ran down her spine as she stiffened and sat straight up at the voice of Greg behind her. She made the choice not to say anything and took another bite from the plate.

"Stopped watching your calories too? I didn't mean to mess you up that bad." Now in front of her, there was little she could do to ignore his presence aside from get up and leave.

"Go away Greg. I have nothing to say to you." She scanned the crowd and looked for Josh again, catching his back still at the buffet as Greg slid into Josh's chair across from her.

"Oh please, we both know you have a lot you want to say. I have to say I am shocked to see you here alone. Figured you'd bring your friend like always, what was her name?"

Hannah knew that he was baiting her, but she didn't have the self-control to stay quiet when he did. Just as she opened her mouth to respond though, Josh cut her off.

"Excuse me, you're in my seat." Josh stood looking impatient with a full plate in his hands.

"You're joking right? You don't have to save her just because the little quiet girl looks lonely." Greg scoffed.

"I'm not. This is my date, Hannah, and you are in my seat. I won't need to inform you of that fact again, will I?"

Of all the things she had pictured about coming up here with Josh, and it was a lot, this wasn't in it. Him squaring off with Greg was something to behold, and she fell harder for him than she had with the kiss earlier.

"Where did she find you? An escort service." Greg looked Josh up and down with a sneer as he stood.

"Better than the trash pile she picked you up from." Josh set down his plate and took his seat across from Hannah, holding her gaze and never looking at Greg, when no response came.

"Oh, you're a funny guy, huh? I'll keep that in mind." Greg threw at him and then waited a beat for Josh to reply before sauntering off to bother someone else.

"You really dated that guy?" Josh paused before adding, "you were going to marry him?" He pulled his face, showing his complete disgust at the idea.

"It made sense at the time." She shrugged her shoulders and pushed the food away, what little appetite she had, now gone. "I'm ready to find our things when you're done."

"Not yet. We won't let him run us off, okay?" He didn't say anything else until Hannah looked at him. "What did he mean by he'll remember that I'm a funny guy?"

She couldn't help it and a small giggle escaped. "He will probably go google scathing insults that people will find funny and hit you with them next time he sees you."

Josh's fork paused halfway to his wide open mouth. He was frozen for a moment before sitting his fork back down. "You're joking?"

Hannah shook her head. "I've seen his search history. It's a lot of things like that."

Unable to contain it anymore, her giggling turned in to an outright laugh, one that she couldn't hold back. It was completely ridiculous, and she knew it, just had never really thought about it before. It didn't take long before Josh was laughing too and suddenly they were both wiping tears as they tried to return to calm.

"That's the best thing I've ever heard. I cannot wait until next time I see him." He pulled out his phone. "Maybe I'll search it myself and try to figure out what he'll say."

The laughter she'd just pushed back down spilled over again. This time Hannah held her stomach, aching from the workout it was getting. "Stop, you're making my stomach hurt."

"Oh, I'm never letting this go." Josh put his phone down and shook his head in disbelief before finally taking the bite of food he'd tried to eat a few minutes ago.

When Josh had finished eating, he and Hannah had headed to the front desk to get the keys to their room and find out where it was exactly. He'd half-expected literal keys just to go with the rustic feel of the resort and was a little disappointed when they'd handed them keycards instead.

Hannah was quiet as they walked to their room and he wondered if it had just occurred to her to think about sleeping arrangements. It had certainly just popped into his mind for the first time. He hoped there wasn't a pull-out sofa bed or anything he could use in there and they'd get to share the bed. *What I wouldn't give to just have her splayed out before me right now.*

Josh cleared his throat and pushed his desires down as he slid the keycard into the slot and unlocked the door to their room. He held it open wide and let Hannah enter first, closing the door behind him and setting the keycard on the small table by the door before taking in the room.

Rustic was what this place was all about and the rooms were no exception. Exposed wood everywhere, the four-poster bed was made out of the same wood as the walls and faced a fireplace. Cozy was the only word for it. On the bed was a quilt in a pattern of greens to look like trees and their luggage was at the foot of the bed. Hannah stood still looking at the bed and jumped when he touched her shoulder.

"I'm sorry, I didn't think about the sleeping arrangements." Her voice quivered a touch, and he knew it was bothering her.

"What's wrong? Do you think I'll fight you for sides of the bed?" He plopped down onto the bed and made a show of getting comfortable. "I guess I could try both sides, but I'm usually a left side kind of guy."

"I mean, I just didn't think about it." Confirming his thoughts from earlier.

"Hannah we are both adults, we can share a bed."

She didn't say anything but walked around to the other side of the bed and opened the curtains. Hannah had always been an internal person, needing to process everything before saying anything and she did it in her own head. He'd watched her do it as long as he'd known her. As much as he'd like to push for a reaction, he knew Hannah would come to terms with things all on her own, while staring out at the mountains again.

Josh got up and checked out the small bathroom before moving the fireplace. It was an electric fireplace tucked inside a brick frame to make it look more like the real thing. He was fine with it not being wood burning as he had no real idea what to do with it if it was. Flip a switch though, he got it.

Sitting on the mantle was a bucket of ice with two bottles of wine and glasses, with a note on the tray. Josh took it down and set it on the small table that was nestled between the two chairs facing the fireplace. The note was addressed to them both but since he knew no one here, he left the note for Hannah and opened a bottle of wine, pouring two glasses.

"Hannah, I poured you a glass, come join me." He beckoned.

She turned from the mountain view then to look at him before he watched the decision get made on her face. She had been about to say no, but for some reason had changed her mind and sat in the other chair. He handed her the glass, and she took it along with the note still sitting on the tray. Reading the note, she turned it over and handed it to him.

It simply thanked them for coming and asked them to have a good time, wine was on the house. "Hannah, really, if you're uncomfortable I will get another room."

"What? No, it's fine. I mean a little weird, but fine. I'm not upset." He could tell that she was though as it all came out as one sentence and faster than he'd ever heard her talk.

"If you say so." Josh tipped his glass back and took a long sip of his own glass. "I'm going to change and shower right quick unless there was something else you wanted to do tonight?" It was going on dark already and he just wanted to change out of these clothes he'd been cramped into the car for 7 hours today in.

"Not that I can think of." Setting down her glass, she rose too. "I'll get my stuff out so I can go after you. It was a long ride up here."

Josh nodded and disappeared into the bathroom before he embarrassed himself just thinking about her showering after him. He needed to take this time to clear his mind. Maybe a cold shower was in order.

In record time, Josh showered, shivered, and got dressed. Hannah was sitting on the bed, leaning against the headboard with her wine in one had and the remote in the other when he emerged from the bathroom.

"All yours."

"Thanks." Rising from the bed she tossed the remote to his side and gathered her clothes. "There was a TV in the armoire over there, so at least it won't be boring tonight, right?"

Josh picked up the remote and nodded as Hannah headed into the bathroom. Now he was just going to sit here with his thoughts and pray he could find something on TV to distract him. After a few minutes though, restlessness took over, and he started to look through the drawers in the room to pass the time.

Hannah had left her things in her suitcase like him, so he had no fear of prying, he did find a room service menu and took it back to the bed to read through it. She was taking a while, so he called in for a large order of cheese fries, knowing she hadn't eaten much today and would never turn those down.

No sooner than he hung up, Hannah opened the door and steam poured out from her shower, bringing with it the scent of her fruity shampoo.

"Is that a menu?" Hannah laughed as she tucked her dirty clothes away. "How are you not full?"

"Sure is, and I was thinking that there's no way you ARE full so I ordered cheese fries."

"Shut the front door! Did you really?"

"Would I lie about such a thing to you?"

"I hope not. I hadn't realized how hungry I was until I was sipping the wine and decided I should slow down."

Josh nodded. Drinking on an empty stomach was never a good idea. He'd thought she'd had another glass or two while he was in the shower, but he noticed now, she'd only poured one and barely sipped on it.

"I didn't think to order something else to drink. Do you want me to call them back?" Josh reached for the phone in the room.

"No, no, it's fine. I can sip this now that I know I'll have some food. Plus there' are a few bottles of water in the mini fridge."

"Mini fridge?" He'd looked the room over but hadn't seen one.

"Right here." Hannah reached down and opened what looked like an end table by the fireplace with a lamp on it. It was a small cabinet though with a fridge behind it.

"This place is unreal. I'm going to come back just to learn all their secrets and pretend to be roughing it while I hide the conveniences. Did you find anything else?"

"Just the TV. I kinda stopped after that though, you were quick in the shower."

"Well, come have a seat, we can explore more tomorrow." Josh patted the bed beside him, and to his surprise she didn't hesitate and sat down, leaning back against the pillows and headboard as she had been before she showered.

She turned to face him. "Thank you so much for this."

"Nothing to thank me for. It's a great place up here." Trying to downplay wherever she was headed with this.

"No, for everything, showing off to my friends when we got here. Running Greg off, just everything."

"Hannah, please don't thank me for anything. Greg's an ass, and someone should have told him so a long time ago." He left the other part out. He wasn't about to bring up the kiss again, when all he wanted was to take her in his arms again and feel her melt into him.

"Well, maybe, but the kiss—"

She didn't get the chance to finish that sentence before Josh decided to show her how much she didn't need to thank him for the kiss. As his mouth hit hers he felt her sigh and her body turn into putty next to him. Taking a chance, he slid one had down her body to her hip and pulled her slightly closer to him.

Hannah complied completely and adjusted herself closer to him and lower in the bed. Needing no further encouragement, Josh moved from her lips to her neck and placed a feather-like kisses down to her collarbone as he readjusted in the bed as well. Now both laying down, Josh was half hovering over her and half on the bed, that one hand wandering back up towards her breasts.

"Josh, please, don't stop."

Crushing the words with his lips he rendered her breathless again with another passionate kiss. A knock on the door made them both pause. Josh shook his head. *What am I doing?* He backed off and adjusted himself as he went to answer the door.

Cheese fries, of course. At least he managed to save himself, however much by accident it was. Josh tipped the lady and carried the fries back to the bed. Hannah was sitting up again and had readjusted her clothes and hair.

"Fries." Josh said weakly.

"Um, great." She scooted over in the bed so he could set them down between them.

He set them down and then climbed in next to her, plate of food between them. Hannah handed him the remote for the TV as she went all in on the fries. He settled on a comedy movie he knew they'd both seen before and then helped himself to a few fries.

It seemed as though she wanted to just avoid what had happened and since he still hadn't wrapped his mind around it, he was fine with that. He knew one thing for sure though, they were going to discuss it before this weekend was over.

CHAPTER 5

*H*annah was warm, relaxed, and comfortable. That was the first thing she thought as her eyes came open the next morning. She tried to stretch only to realize something was holding her down and in this position. That's when it hit her.

It wasn't something hold her in place, it was someone. Josh's arm was draped across her middle and he was flush against her back, the source of her warmth no doubt. Hannah resisted the urge to nestle back into his warmth but made no movement to get up either. She was going to lay here and enjoy while she could.

Memories of last night flooded back into her mind, the steaming kiss and the almost something more. She wished now that they had done more, but knew it was for the best if they didn't. He was her best friend's brother after all, and she'd known him forever.

Only none of that really mattered to her. If she was being honest, she'd also had the hots for him forever as well. Unmoving, she laid there and embraced the comforting warmth he was giving her and tried to focus on the mountains outside the window.

Josh moved behind her and Hannah kept herself very still waiting to see what he did and was completely surprised by the kisses he started placing on her neck.

"Josh, we can't." Hannah moaned.

"Why not?" He whispered in her ear.

"We just shouldn't." Only she didn't move, couldn't move. "If we don't get up though, we will miss breakfast."

"Okay, fine. To be continued then." It wasn't a question, it was a statement, just a fact in his mind.

I'll have to keep myself busy today to keep my mind off of him. That was the only way she would get through the day. For now, no thinking about tonight. If she thought about tonight already, she would panic and not be able to get through the day.

They both quietly moved around and got ready for breakfast. Another buffet style service was set up for them when they got there. A few people remained but as it was getting late in the morning, most had likely already come and gone. As they sat, Sara quickly joined them.

"Good morning guys, I hope you slept well." She grabbed the empty chair next to Hannah and sat.

"Best nights sleep I've had in a while." Josh added a wink to Hannah.

Blushing, Hannah changed the subject. "Are you ready for tomorrow?" She shoved a bite of eggs in her mouth to keep from saying anything else.

"Don't be embarrassed Hannah, it's nice to see you so happy. And yes, I am ready for tomorrow, I think. I will let you eat your breakfast, don't forget the rehearsal later and then the dinner. Oh, and I booked us spa time before the rehearsal." Sara set a paper schedule down on the table as she rose.

"Thanks Sara." Hannah smiled.

"I'll chat with you later. You," she looked at Josh, "will have to find other ways to entertain yourself as I will have Hannah today." Sending her own wink towards Josh before walking to another table.

"I guess you are off the hook on our to be continued until much later." Josh took her itinerary that Sara had left at the table. "Well, it looks like we have one hour if you want to return to the room first?" Wiggling his eyebrows, he laughed as Hannah snatched the paper back.

"I told you we can't." Hannah said at a loud whisper, hoping no one heard her.

"You didn't say why. We are two consenting adults after all."

"It's not that I don't want to... what about your sister?"

"I'm wondering if this was a setup for us."

"What?" Choking on her drink she did her best to squash the coughing for the second time this week because of him, as people turned to look at her. "You can't seriously think that."

Josh raised both eyebrows at her suggesting it was more odd that she didn't think it. He did have a fair point; Grace had always thought herself a matchmaker. It is something she would do. *Double damn.* This would require more thought and a conversation with Grace.

Rising, Josh kissed her forehead. "Have a good day. I'm going to go see what I can get into and you need to do whatever women do to get ready for a spa day." Smiling he walked away leaving Hannah sitting there with all her thoughts.

This wasn't the place to sit and reflect though, so she left the dining room too and headed for their room to change and get ready for the list of things Sara wanted to do. She had a full day packed into the afternoon before the rehearsal from mani pedis to massages. At least she knew she'd be too busy to stress about Josh.

She changed and sent off a quick text to Grace before heading down to the spa. The more she thought about things and waited for a text back from Grace, the more she thought Josh might be right. If that was the case, not only was she a little mad at Grace, she was also reconsidering her resolution not to do anything with Josh tonight.

"Hannah!" Sara waved from one of the rooms in the spa as Hannah arrived.

"Sara! This is going to be just what I need this weekend." She slid into the pedicure chair next to her.

"Well, we need the details on that sexy boyfriend of yours."

Nope, not what I needed. Turns out it would be a very long day instead of the relaxing one she wanted.

"I mean there's really not much to say." Trying to skirt around any real answers she continued, "what color are you thinking for our toes?"

"We are doing the ice blue on our toes and just French tips for our fingernails." Sara showed her the blue color for their toes. "Now, about Josh."

"We've known each other for a while and after Greg and I... broke up, he was just there for me." Shrugging she concentrated on the massage chair instead as her feet soaked.

"Well, he looks good on you and I'm glad to see you happy." Sara reached over and squeezed her hand before returning to talk of the wedding as the other bridesmaids arrived and took their seats as well.

Hannah was grateful that apart from a few more questions Sara had let it go about Josh. She was able to relax and just enjoy her time with her friends from college that she hadn't seen in a long time. She would have loved to stay there with them longer, just catching up, but the rehearsal was approaching.

The four women went their separate ways shortly before the dinner was to start and Hannah headed for their room, hoping to run into Josh for just a minute. The room was empty when she reached it and it didn't look like anything had been moved, even the bed was still neat. He must have found something to do today. It shouldn't have disappointed her, but it did.

On the way to the rehearsal Hannah thought about why she was disappointed at not seeing him when her goal had been to avoid him. She knew though. Knew that she had made up her mind and wasn't going to let this time go with him. Knew that tonight she wouldn't think of Grace or what shouldn't happen, she would just enjoy herself.

Happy with herself, she was still smiling when the wedding planner told her where to stand and wait. She was just going through the motions until she saw Greg and his sneer directed to her. Thankfully she wouldn't have to walk down with Greg, the less interaction with him the better.

Funny thing was that she had forgotten all about him. Her entire reason for bringing Josh with her was to show up to Greg, and at some point in the last 24 hours that had stopped being important. Instead she looked past Greg now to scan the seats for Josh, not seeing him from her viewpoint.

The rest of the rehearsal was pretty much as she expected it and she knew the moment that Josh had entered even though she had her back to the seats. She had felt him enter the room and then her whole body had felt warm and comfortable like this morning and she knew he was staring at her.

Her smile was bright as the practiced walking out after the ceremony and she waited outside the doors for Josh. She couldn't quell it as she saw him walk towards her. In that moment she decided not to be the one waiting and met him in the middle of the large hallway.

"Hey, you look like you had a good time today." Josh greeted.

No words would do for what she had to say to him. Instead she put her hand on the back of his neck and pulled him toward her for a breathtaking kiss. She was rewarded when she felt Josh's arms come around her and pull her tighter to him. Hannah pulled back to take him in and saw him smiling down at her.

"I don't know what that was for, but I wish you had gone to the spa yesterday."

"I guess I just realized what I had turned down and thought about how dumb I was being." Hannah bit her lip and hoped he hadn't changed his mind.

"In that case, do you think we can skip this dinner business?"

"You? Skip food?" She laughed and shook her head.

Leaning down he whispered, "there's always room service."

"True." Laughing again, she backed out of his embrace. "However, I don't think this dinner is optional."

"Okay, we should eat a lot of carbs, we're going to need the energy." Winking he took her hand as the walked to the dining room for the rehearsal dinner.

"Promises, promises." Hannah winked back and enjoyed the happiness that had settled over her.

CHAPTER 6

Josh's foot bounced up and down as he waited on the rehearsal dinner to be over. Already an hour had passed, and he was ready to grab Hannah and run from the room but doing his best to pretend he had patience. After Hannah's words earlier he couldn't concentrate on anything and was glad there weren't his friends, so he wasn't expected to participate in any conversations in full.

Hannah reached under the table and rested her hand on his thigh, startling him. Josh's leg jumped up so high his knee hit the table causing glasses to rattle. As everyone looked around for the reason for the disturbance, he caught Hannah out the corner of his eye trying to stifle her laughter and doing a poor job of it.

After a moment the party resumed their chatters with only a few people waggling their eyebrows at Josh and Hannah. Breathing a sigh of relief, he reached below the table as well and held on to her hand, before it went rogue and really embarrassed them here at the table. Hannah continued to grin and shake as she silently laughed.

"Is it an acceptable time to leave yet?" He leaned over and whispered in her ear.

Hannah shivered before replying. "Not yet, almost, they're going to thank everyone for coming and then we can go."

"Your friends seem happy you're here with me. I doubt they would mind if we skipped out."

Hannah squeezed his thigh where her hand was still burning through his pants and searing his skin. Sara and Paul stood and gave a short speech exactly as Hannah had predicted. When they were through, the happy couple left the room and the rest of the guests began spilling out behind them.

"You know, it's rude to be fooling around at the table with so many people present, or any others really." Greg's harsh tone had Josh stopping in his tracks.

"Dude, if that's what we were doing everyone would have known. Go worry about yourself and leave us alone." Hannah surprised both men with her harsh-toned response to Greg before tugging Josh along and leaving Greg standing there with his mouth open.

"Everyone would have known, huh?" Josh asked when they were out of earshot of Greg.

"We will find out if I was lying or not very soon."

"A challenge? Hmm, I hope you're prepared for this."

Hannah just laughed as they continued their trek to the room. Was it just him or did it seem farther away tonight? Maybe it was just his anticipation building that was making the whole night drag on, but they couldn't get there fast enough.

Hannah opened the door to the room and Josh wasted no more time. Kicking the door closed behind him he spun Hannah against it and kissed her like he was a dying man and she was his cure.

Out of breath, he released her mouth and moved his lips to her neck as his hands gripped her ass, lifting her off the floor, using the door for support Josh returned his assault to her mouth as Hannah moaned into him.

"Hold on to me." Josh panted, determined to get her from the door to the bed.

Hannah complied, wrapping tightly around him with her legs and arms, she leaned back down for more kissing. Both out of breath, they fell onto the bed together, Josh immediately moving to pull her dress up.

"Stop." Hannah said between breaths.

Josh had never frozen so quickly in his life. *Was she changing her mind right now?* Josh backed away from her, prepared to do what she wanted and stop.

Hannah looked up confused at him. "Don't go away, I just wanted to see you."

"I'm right here."

Hannah slid more onto the bed and look back at Josh through her heavy-lidded eyes. "All of you."

Dawning struck Josh like a bolt of lightning and he immediately began to undress. She wanted a show? He would damn sure give it to her. Shirts first, tossed to the side, Josh never took his eyes off of her as he stepped out of his shoes and unbuttoned his pants.

Hannah bit her lip as she watched him and slowly slipped her panties off from under her dress. *The tease.* Josh nearly tripped as he pulled his pants off and tried to shake them free from his legs. Expecting her to be laughing at him, he climbed onto the bed, boxers still on.

Instead she watched every move he made, and never looked away, no amusement anywhere to be found as he searched her face. She stood and pulled the dress over her head revealing her naked glory for him before climbing back into the bed and pushing Josh to lay fully down as she climbed on top of him.

Josh groaned as she slid his boxers slowly down, the lightest of touches on his cock as she did so. Fully removing them, Hannah slowly dragged her hand back up his leg, finally wrapping it fully around his length.

His eyes rolled back as he pushed his head back into the pillow. A hiss escaped his lips as his little tease surprised him again and took him into her mouth. Josh gripped the sheets on either side of his body to keep himself from grabbing her or being too rough. She wanted to explore him, he would let her.

Taking a chance, Josh lifted his head to watch her as she sucked, only to find that her eyes were on his face already and her other hand was otherwise occupied. "That is not how we do this." In one swift movement Josh had tipped her back and covered her with his own body.

Hannah's husky laughter told him she was ready for the same thing he was. All of it. Josh left her in the bed long enough to grab a condom from his bag and roll it on. She watched him as he did and somehow he got impossibly harder. Unable to stand it any longer, he climbed back into the bed and Hannah's legs wrapped around him immediately.

Positioning himself at her entrance, Josh hesitated, giving her one last chance to change her mind, knowing this had been a hard decision for her. *God help me, I don't know what I'll do if she does.* Instead, Hannah used her ankles to drive him forward while pulling herself upwards.

A moan escaped them both as Josh leaned over her and plunged himself to the hilt within her heat. As he began to move, more moans slipped from Hannah and was sure she had no idea. Knowing he wouldn't last long, Josh leaned his head down and took one pert nipple into his mouth. To his delight her heard Hannah's breath catch before one hand, gripping his hair, holding his head to her breast.

Josh suckled as he pumped, and she matched his rhythm perfectly. He moved to her other breast and felt her begin to tighten around him. With one final nip of her nipple, he pulled away to watch as she fell over the edge of her release. Watching her face as she came was an aphrodisiac like no other and Josh fell with her, both crying out as they finally reached the peak.

He collapsed on top of her, placing gentle kisses on her collarbone before rolling away. Hannah didn't move as he rose and tossed the condom in the garbage. Returning to the bed, her eyes were already closed, and he scooped her up and placed her right side up in the bed before climbing in next to her and pulling the covers up around them both.

Struggling to stay awake, Josh tried to take in all that had happened tonight and the intensity of it. Pulling her close against him, Josh smiled, thoughts of him perfectly she fit against him whirling around as he finally slept.

CHAPTER 7

Hannah's alarm went off, bringing her out of a delightful dream. She smiled and stretched as Josh moved to find her phone.

"Why in the world is this going off?" He groaned as he climbed back in bed, handing her the phone.

"It's Sara's wedding day. I have to go down and start getting ready." Her words didn't reflect her actions though as she rolled towards Josh and curled up in the crook of his arm.

"You better get moving then." Josh rubbed her back as she struggled between needing to move and never wanting to again.

"Fine." Hannah groaned and climbed out of the bed, taking the sheet with her. Grabbing her clothes from her suitcase, she slipped into the bathroom to shower.

By the time she was ready, Josh had completely cleaned the room. Gone were the clothes strewn all over the place, gone was the messy bed, and, much to her dismay, gone was Josh. It was like nothing had happened. If it weren't for her deliciously sore muscles, she'd wonder if it did.

Hannah slipped the sheet she had worn earlier into one of the chairs and went back to her suitcase. Pulling out her shoes for today and slipping on her sandals, she moved to the closet and pulled out her bridesmaid dress. *Thank God Sara has good taste and I'm not wearing something insane.*

Josh came back to the room as she placed everything on the bed, preparing to head down to meet Sara.

"I got coffee." Josh held up a cup as he shut the door and carried it to her. Shocking her, Josh held onto it, instead leaning down for another knee-weakening kiss that had Hannah sitting down on the bed because standing was no longer something she was capable of. "Good morning." He said as he backed away.

"Good morning indeed." Grinning, she took the coffee and immediately downed a few sips before returning to her mental list of what she needed to bring with her.

"Are you all getting ready together?"

She nodded, wishing she had the morning to lounge around with him before they left after the wedding. Not wanting to take off extra time from work, she had only planned on staying until today, but she would rather stay another night now.

"If you pack up everything you won't need, I'll make sure the car gets loaded up while you're busy this morning."

So many things went through her mind in response. Questions about what happened next with them, but she pushed them all away for now, wanting to enjoy this while it was happening, whatever it was.

"I'm just about done actually, I need to head down soon to meet everyone else."

"I'll get this wrapped up in here then and shower." He stopped and turned back to her. "What time is the wedding ceremony?"

"It's at eleven this morning, you just go in and grab a seat and I will meet with you after it's over."

"Isn't that early for a wedding?"

"It's also on a Sunday, which is a little odd. Sara said yesterday that they had other things booked and this was the only time they had to accommodate them."

"I see, and since Paul wouldn't go anywhere else for the ceremony…" Shaking his head, Josh let that hang in the air. They both knew it had likely been an argument between the two.

"Okay, I am heading down. All my things are packed over there." Hannah pointed towards her small stack of bags.

"Great, I'll get it loaded up." He looked like he was going to say more but then stopped.

Hannah waited a moment to see if he would continue. When nothing else was said she left the room, thoughts of what next going with her.

Getting ready was distracting to say the very least. The whole time up to the start of the ceremony Sara had been a complete mess. She panicked over every little thing and had to be calmed down constantly. They ended up taking turns with her trying to keep her calm.

Even her worrisome thoughts about Josh had subsided thanks to Sara. Until the ceremony that is. Josh was dressed to the nines in a suit and tie that she had never seen before and she found it hard to take her eyes off of him as she walked down the aisle.

Her eyes were immediately back on him as she took her place. It was hard to look away as he grinned back at her and suddenly her light blue strapless dress turned into fire, because she was being burned alive by his gaze.

Once the ceremony was over, they headed to the reception where she was finally able to spot Josh in the crowd after a little looking around. "Hey stranger," she said as she approached.

"I've been looking for you." Turning Josh wrapped both arms around her and picked her up to spin her as they kissed there in front of everyone.

"I talked to my sister earlier." He said as he set her down. *Why would he bring her up now?* "And?"

"Well, I just wanted to make sure that if we decided not to make this just a weekend fling that she wouldn't mind."

Hannah swatted his arm, the long pauses between each piece of information were getting to her. "And?"

"She said she was hoping that we would realize we were meant for each other."

The breath she'd been holding whooshed out at once as she relaxed with that answer. "So, does that mean you want to be more than a weekend fling?"

"Like maybe several weekend flings?" Winking, he grinned even wider, showing his dimples he liked to hide, as she playfully swatted his arm again. "Yes, I want to give us as a couple a real chance."

Hannah nodded and wrapped both her arms around his neck as she pulled him down to kiss her. "There's nothing I want more."

THE END

THE WEDDING RUSE

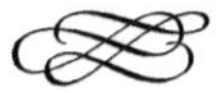

CHAPTER 1

It was definitely going to be a long weekend. Skipping out on the wedding she was supposed to attend with her friend Hannah was just the latest thing she was adding to the list of reasons why she needed to stop hanging out with Tristan. The other reason was that she wasn't hanging out with Tristan either, she was working with him, kinda.

Tristan Munson was an architect, a damn good one at that. Grace was a photographer and she'd been helping him on the side here and there to help him get a better feel for areas. He told her that her photos helped him capture something he couldn't see on his own. The fact that he paid didn't hurt, but the fact that she melted every time he called was the real reason.

She'd met him through work, as a marketing photographer, she had shot material for his architecture firm. That had been nearly a year ago and she was still putty each time the phone rang. He probably didn't even know, and she was stupid to feel anything for him as he'd not made a single move towards her in the time, she'd known him. She definitely shouldn't have skipped out on Hannah for this.

Grace threw several outfits on the bed as she decided what to wear now that Josh had left to pick up Hannah, she had the apartment to herself and could obsess over what to wear. Something she could move around in wasn't always the most flattering of things. Normally she would have Hannah help her, but Hannah didn't know about Tristan. She didn't want to hear all the reasons, the very logical ones, about why she shouldn't drop everything for this guy that didn't see her, only her work.

The ironic part of all of this was she wanted to be recognized for her work. It was a tough business and she craved nothing more, aside from Tristan to notice her. Tossing tops to the floor, she decided today was going to be the day she did more than blend in like she normally did for sessions. Today she was going to stand out.

Outfit decided, she quickly got dressed, did her makeup and hair. Only then did she realize she still had two hours before she needed to meet him, and it would only take about 25 minutes to get there at the longest.

Pacing wasn't cutting it and checking her phone wasn't either. Several times a minute she glanced at it and it was taking forever for a single minute to pass. She dropped herself onto the couch and double checked she had all the lenses she needed, back up battery, and anything else she could think of.

Pacing was getting old. She grabbed a drink from the fridge and sat down at the bar with her laptop, looking through the emails again for any clue about where they might be going. He had only asked her to meet him at his firm and they would head out together. She didn't even know what kind of photos they were taking.

What if I should blend in? What if I need better shoes?

Glancing at her feet didn't help. She wasn't dressed right for taking photos of an unknown subject. Sighing, she knew she needed to change.

It took no time to grab her black slacks, plain top, and sensible shoes. She carefully hung back up the pretty skirt and blouse she intended to wear. If she couldn't do her job, he wouldn't call her anymore anyway. With one last look at her cute heels, she put them back in the box, and back in her closet. Another time.

A buzzing phone pulled her from her thoughts. Expecting it to be Hannah, she didn't rush to answer it. She had no intention of answering her this weekend. She felt bad, but those two needed to spend a little time together so she would be able to stop seeing stolen glances at each other.

Her mouth fell open as she made it to the phone just as it stopped ringing. Missed call from Tristan. Before she could debate calling him back, it rang again.

"Hello?" No longer worried about wrinkling her outfit, she fell onto the sofa.

"Hey, I have a proposition for you."

I have one for you, too. She shook her head to clear that thought out before replying. "What's up?"

"I know I didn't give you much to go on, but do you think you could pack a bag for a night or two?"

"Umm," hell yes, I can spend the night with you. Ugh, that's definitely not what he is saying. "That depends on where we are going and really how long."

"Well," she heard him lean back, could imagine him settle into his chair and could practically see him run his long fingers through his hair. "You can't back out now though, promise?"

"You pay too well for me to do that." She joked.

"You say that, but what if I told you that this is a completely different project that our normal ones?"

"I had already guessed as much, so spill. I'm not going to back out."

"It's a ranch."

She waited, but he didn't add anything else. "Like horses?"

"Yeah, animals, a lodge, bunks."

"What—" She didn't even know what to ask.

"Look, my uncle owns it, I want to give everything a facelift, make it more family friendly and help him get some things going. I know it's not a normal request."

"Okay? What exactly am I taking pictures of?"

"I don't know." He let out a deep breath. "I never do though, you always figure it out."

"This isn't my normal subject though, I don't know—"

"I will explain everything else on the way. Do you mind staying a night or two though? It's also much bigger area than our normal projects."

"Yeah, sure. Let me change and pack and I will head out." Her head was spinning but she rose and went to her room.

"I'll pick you up instead, shortly."

Grace nodded before she remembered it was a phone call. "Yeah, okay."

Dropping the phone onto the couch she stared at it. This was not what she expected. Now what? Torn between excitement and nervousness, she chewed her lip before jumping up and changing her clothes, again.

CHAPTER 2

Tristan ran his hand through his hair as he pulled up to Grace's building. He had second guessed this plan since he'd made it earlier this week. He really just wanted to spend some time with her, but this may not have been the smartest idea.

It wasn't that he didn't have work to do for his uncle, who was out of town this weekend, he didn't know how she would react to him asking her to stay up there with him. He still didn't know how she felt. Yeah, he was paying her, but she didn't seem upset. Shocked was more how he would describe it.

Before he could get out of the car, Grace was already tapping on his window, pulling him from his thoughts. He climbed out and went to meet her at the trunk, popping it as he went.

"Let me get those, I would have met you upstairs, you know?" Tristan said as he grabbed her suitcase from her.

"It's not a big deal. I didn't think you would be long, so I tried to hurry and get down here." She said, in the way that she normally did, quiet and rarely looking at him.

"I didn't mean for you to rush; I would have waited."

"It's okay."

Walking with her to her door, he opened it for her, watching her as she took her seat. She looked different today. Instead of her usual blend in clothes, she was in jeans and a sweater. He liked her better in her normal clothes, he realized. The way the jeans molded to her was a bonus over those flowy black pants she always wore.

"That's everything" She said.

He was still standing there with the door open and hadn't even noticed. Shaking his head at himself, he closed it and then got in himself.

"You can be the DJ." And just like that they were on the way to spending a weekend together.

Grace hadn't moved the entire time they were on the road or said anything. She hadn't even asked him about what the project was. After about an hour, he couldn't take it anymore.

"I won't bite."

She looked up at him with the cutest confused face before turning red and looking back at her feet. "I know."

"You're very quiet, we can talk." She didn't say anything, so he started. "So, my uncle has this like dude ranch type thing."

No response again. He always forgot how quiet she was. He didn't know if maybe he was annoying her, so didn't add anything else to it. After about five minutes he barely heard her start talking.

"What are you doing there?"

"I am working on redoing a few of the older buildings for him. Seeing if there is any way to make them work better and what might need to stay the same."

Out of the corner of his eye, he saw her nod. Taking that as encouragement to continue the conversation, he did.

"Some of the buildings have been there for so long I can't even give you a date. Others are newer, but things just aren't flowing right."

"Makes sense." She never looked back at him but stopped looking at her feet and was back to looking out the window.

"He's closed right now, always takes a week off in the fall to do his own travelling. So, he's left us the key to one of the little bunks, for us to use." He waited to see if she would respond at all or even tense at the knowledge they were staying alone together. She didn't react at all.

"Have you ridden horses? We can while we are there if you want."

She shook her head, and he only noticed because her short curls bounced as she did so. "I've never ridden, so probably not a good idea."

"I may just sell you on it. You never know." Tristan hoped a little teasing would bring her out of her shell a little.

This time when she got quiet, he left her alone to her thoughts. Which left him to his own thoughts.

She was always so quiet around him and he didn't really understand it. Suddenly a pit settled in the bottom of his stomach. *What if she doesn't like me at all?* This was going to put a real damper on his weekend if it was because she was only tolerating him, rather than actually liking his company.

But that couldn't be it. She spoke to him on the phone most of the time, and there was no attitude like she wanted off the phone. Her emails were even more wordy. He'd definitely read way more words from her than he had heard her speak.

Then again, whenever anyone else came up to her while doing photos, she always had plenty to talk about. He let out a small groan before he could stop it. Sitting up taller, he pretended it was just from the car ride.

By the time they pulled up to the lodge, he was fairly

certain she had fallen asleep. She hadn't said another word, even when he turned the radio on. He had given up on attempts at conversation completely.

Parking the car, he reached over and touched her leg, planning to shake it to wake her a little. Instead she jumped and squeaked. He couldn't help it, and the laughter than threatened spilled over.

"I'm sorry, I thought you were asleep." Tristan barely got the words out between deep breaths and laughing.

"I'm not." She was red again, clearly embarrassed.

"I didn't mean to startle you, really."

"I know." She was back to looking at the floor.

"Hey, look at me, please?" It took her a second, but she finally did turn and make eye contact with him. "I really am sorry."

"It's really okay. I was just lost in my thoughts."

Nodding, he opened the door and stretched as he climbed out of the small car. He loved his car, especially for the gas mileage, but his 6-foot frame didn't like being in it for too long.

Grace walked with him into the lodge. Looking every-where but at him as she did. She appeared to like what she saw though as she seemed to be in awe of everything. Her eyes were as big as quarters as she took it all in. He let himself behind the counter and rummaged through things for the envelope his uncle said would be there.

"This is amazing." She was standing in the middle of the lodge, just spinning around.

"I'm glad you like it, it's the biggest building out here."

"Are you changing this one?"

"Nope, we all like it the way it is. It's nice and open." He gestured towards the rows of picnic tables that led the way to the massive fireplace. "He likes that all the families or people that stay here can interact with each other.

"Good."

A grin spread its way across his face. He hadn't realized how important it was to him that she liked it. He was proud of this place that he had grown up as a part of. Still smiling he led her back out of the lodge and to the car.

CHAPTER 3

This place was amazing. It was rustic, definitely a ranch, or looked like she thought one should, and not something she ever would have imagined here. Even though she lived in New York State, she was still one of those people that didn't think much out of the city.

Mentally kicking herself all the way up the road for not attempting any conversations with Tristan was completely forgotten when she walked inside. Her only thought now was to get Tristan in jeans and a cowboy hat by that fireplace was all she wanted to see through her camera lense now.

The bunk as he called it was another five-minute drive down a gravel road, or path, more of a path. From where the lodge. It hadn't escaped her notice that she was supposed to be in an entirely different kind of lodge with Hannah this weekend either. Checking her phone, no service, guess they were really on their own.

"We are in the one to the right." Tristan pointed at one of the two cabins in front of them.

"Cool, I'll grab my bags."

"Just wait, we will go take a look around, make sure there are no issues before we do."

Nodding, she waited for him to unlock the door and they walked through. "I am not sure what bunk means to you, but this is not what I expected."

"There are other ones, we can try a different one." Tristan turned to walk out.

"Not at all what I mean. This is so pretty." She turned and took in the small room. "I thought more like a bunkroom with actual bunk beds or something."

Tristan laughed. "There are two rooms in here, and the kitchen and living room. Of course, a bathroom as well."

"Which room did you want?"

"You choose, you are doing me a favor staying here."

Grace took the opportunity to walk away from Tristan and the overwhelming presence he had and explored the first room. A decent size queen bed sat in the middle of the room, unadorned. A plain blue blanket was on it, tan sheets. It seemed as simple as everything else she had seen so far, but it worked.

A quick peek out the room to see where Tristan was, first, she checked the other room and found it to be much the same, just on opposite walls. The bathroom was between the two rooms. Nothing fancy there either.

"Did you choose?"

Grace jumped, again. She didn't know why he had her so on edge, maybe it was being so alone with him.

He laughed again. "I promise I am not trying to scare you."

"It's not your fault, I guess I am a little jumpy today."

"You didn't have to stay if you didn't want. Or I can get another set of keys for me to stay in another bunk."

She didn't want him to leave. It definitely wasn't that, she just never knew how to act around him. He made her nervous because she was so turned on and flustered by how attractive he was.

"No, it's not that. I don't know what it is. You're fine." He raised an eyebrow as if to ask her if she was sure. "Honestly I would probably be terrified to stay here on my own."

"If you're sure?"

"I am. You can put the things down in that room. Thank you for carrying it in."

"I do know how to be a gentleman." Winking at her as he walked into her room.

That wink did things that it shouldn't have for the simple thing that it was. It probably, definitely, meant nothing, but tell that to her legs, she instantly turned to jelly at the motion.

Once she recovered her senses, she forced herself to follow him into the room. A deep breath later and she nearly had a grip on herself.

"I am going to go change in the other room and we will grab some lunch from town. You might want to bring your camera, and I will show you around after we eat."

Not trusting herself to talk after thoughts of him changing clothes ran through her mind, she just nodded, again. He smiled and grabbed his bag and walked to the other room and closed the door.

She swallowed hard, staring at the closed door. Never having seen him anything other than business clothes, always long sleeves, she was immediately picturing any number of things that he might consider appropriate to wear at a ranch.

Get it together. She spun away from the door, trying to forget what was going on in the next room. Her eyes caught her camera bag and she carried it into the front room which was the kitchen and living area.

There was one small sofa, more of an oversized chair really, and a small table with two chairs. Other than that, there was a small kitchen area, no electronics outside of the lights and microwave. It just might be a long weekend with nothing to distract herself from him.

She heard Tristan open the door and turned towards the sound. She had not pictured him looking as hot as he did in jeans and a plain t-shirt. She licked her lips in reaction and immediately threw her gaze to the floor. He had to have seen her. She could feel the heat creeping up her face, again. She was going to spend this entire weekend mortified at this rate.

He had muscles, very defined ones, that the shirt hugged them perfectly. That vision was stuck in her head forever and she wasn't the least bit mad about it. And the man in jeans? She'd never seen that before and was definitely here for it.

"What do you think?"

Grace only just managed to pull her eyes off the floor to look at him, only to see him put a cowboy hat on his head. She was lost. Stuck. Couldn't pull her eyes away, even as she felt her mouth fall open.

Her eyes landed on his and she saw something change. There was a heat there, an intensity that she hadn't seen before today. Then again, she rarely made eye contact with him. Slowly a proud smile spread across his face and he tipped the hat at her.

Spinning around she grabbed her bag. "Lunch?"

"Sounds good to me."

The ride to pick up food was short, but she had to give him credit, he hadn't mentioned that he caught her staring at him. She caught him out of the corner of her eye looking at her now and then as they ate, but he didn't mention anything.

They ate their burgers and fries at a small restaurant, and he refused to let her pay for hers. As they rose to leave, he took her hand to help her stand. Completely unnecessary, but not unwelcome. She smiled at him and went to take her hand back after she stood, only to find a strong grip on the other end.

She didn't say a word. Didn't know what this was about but would enjoy it anyway. Even if it never happened again. They walked together to the car and he didn't let go until he had opened the door and she was getting into the car.

Smiling, she buckled in as he shut her door and climber in the other side. She still didn't have the nerve to really look up at him, but through her lashes, she could see a smug smile on his face too. That knowledge only made hers grow.

CHAPTER 4

Tristan didn't even try to hide his smile as he drove her back to the ranch. He was more than pleased with himself. Not only had Grace been truly checking him out after he changed, but she'd let him hold her hand. He'd made a move and it had gone as good as he ever could have imagined. He would wear this hat all day everyday if it made her jaw drop.

She was currently back to being shy, but she was smiling. He could feel more than see her look at him through her lashes every now and then. He wanted to reach over and put his hand on her knee, but he didn't want to take it too far yet.

They pulled back up to their bunk and she shot him a confused look.

"Everything at the ranch is walking distance from here. Maybe a little long of a walk, but I thought you might like to get a look at the whole thing the way guests would. You can leave your camera in the bunk if you want. We have all day tomorrow for work."

"If you're sure?"

"You know I wouldn't say it if I didn't."

She nodded and got out of the car. He unlocked the door and let her put her camera bag away. The reality was he just wanted to walk with her again, see if he could pick up her hand again as they walked. There would really be plenty of time, a full day, to take pictures tomorrow.

She locked the door as she walked through, and he led the way down a path between the bunks. Grace stayed behind him until he finally slowed his pace and dropped in next to her. He slyly grabbed her hand and was pleased to find that she held his back and didn't try to pull away.

He pointed everything out as they walked, the sides of each building and what they were as far as they could see from the path. His goal right now was to get to the stables. There would be people about as the ranch might be closed to the public, but the animals still required care.

They arrived at the fence and he stopped to let her look at the horses that were in the yard milling around. She dropped his hand and put both her arms on the fence as she watched the horses.

"I've never been this close to a horse before." She sounded amazed.

"Wanna go get closer to them?"

"Not yet."

"I won't make you."

"I know." She turned and sent him a reassuring smile. "I want to, but it's weird to see them this close already an realize how big they really are. Now I do wish I had brought my camera."

"I'm sorry."

"Don't be. Just promise me we will come back for me to get some photos before we leave."

"It's a promise." He smiled at her, but she was already watching the horses again.

"Hey folks. How's it going?" Came a man's voice walking up behind them.

"Pretty good." Tristan turned and shook his hand.

"Tristan! Hey man, how have you been?"

"Hey Blake, pretty good."

"Introduce me to this pretty lady you brought with you."

Tristan wanted to grab her and pull her to his side and growl MINE. Instead he offered introductions. Finding himself extremely jealous of the full conversation she was offering to Blake about horses when he had to pry pieces of conversation from her.

"Right, Tristan?"

"What?" He made himself focus on the conversation he had lost track of.

Laughter came from both Blake and Grace and he really wanted to run the man off.

"I was telling Grace here about how when you were younger you used to go swimming in the horse trough over there."

"Yeah, it was pretty normal back then. Pretty sure you were there a time or two."

Grace looked back and forth between them but mostly kept her attention focused on Blake. Tired of sharing her attention, Tristan decided it was time to end it. "You still got chores to work on?" he threw at the man.

"Nope mostly done for the day. Just have to let the horses back in later and get them bedded down. Soon likely, if the weather forecast is right." He turned his attention to Grace, wanna ride one?"

"Not yet, thank you."

Ha! Not with you! He didn't know where this sudden jealous streak had come from, but there was not stuffing it back down now.

"Have you ridden one?" Grace shook her head. "Awe, you

don't know what you're missing. I would be happy to bring you up with me if you're interested."

Grace blushed and glanced at Tristan. "I am good, thank you anyway."

"Well, if you change your mind at all while you're here, or any other time for that matter, you just let me know. I'd be happy to take you for a ride any time."

There was no mistaking the real meaning behind Blake's words and the only thing that saved him from getting punched in the face over it, was the fact that Grace stepped even closer to Tristan. He dropped his hand to his sides, and with considerable effort, managed to uncurl his fists. As he did, he felt Grace's hand slide into his.

All jealousy drained from his body, leaving him with only a rage towards the man that had made her uncomfortable. And behind that, was a pride in her choosing him and seeking him for comfort.

"I think that's enough, Blake. She said no." Tristan managed to get through his gritted teeth.

Blake threw up his hands in mock surrender. "Chill, it was just an offer. I see what's happening here. I wasn't aware there was something between you." He tipped his hat and strolled off towards the stables.

Tristan looked down at Grace, her free hand was wrapped across her body, holding her other arm, closing herself off.

"I'm sorry he might have gotten the wrong impression. I don't do well with being hit on." Shrugging, she pulled at her hand.

"No, he didn't." Tristan pulled at her hand until she was up against him and wrapped his arms around her. "I'm sorry I let him keep talking. I was busy being jealous and didn't notice that you were getting uncomfortable."

At the word jealous she tensed up but had put her arms around him and didn't drop them. "Jealous?"

"You talked to him. You never want to talk to me. I have to ask questions and hope you answer." It was the truth, not the conversation he intended to get into today, or any time soon, but there it was.

Softly, barely audible, he heard her say, "you make me nervous."

Tristan put his hands on her shoulders and pushed her away from him so he could see her. "What does that mean?"

"It's just that…" she twisted her hands and looked at the ground again.

He took one hand off her should and gently cupped her chin, nudging her to look at him. "What?"

"You make me nervous." She tried to put her head back down again, embarrassed she had said it.

"Why?"

"Because. I don't know. Because you're you?"

"What does that mean?" Tristan dropped his hands away from her. "Do I make you uncomfortable?" He had never intended to do that. He took a step back to give her space.

"Yes." She bit her lip. "No, not like that. Not like Blake just did. It's more that I just." She put her gaze back to the ground. "It's that you're so good looking and I forget what to say, and get nervous, and then I don't know what to do."

Everything came out in a rush, and if he wasn't already used to listening to her be so quiet, he never would have heard her. As it was, he wasn't sure he did.

Cupping her chin and urging her to look at him, he struggled to find his own words. When she finally did look up at him and he saw the worry in her eyes, there was no question he had heard her.

He didn't think about his next move. It was natural,

instinct, and all he had wanted for a while now. He leaned down to her and took her mouth in his.

Grace stiffened at first, but it didn't take her long to throw her arms around his neck and give herself fully over to this kiss. Tristan only deepened the kiss as he wrapped his arms around her and pulled her closer to him.

Tristan wasn't sure how long they stood there, next to a wooden fence, with a few horses as an audience, kissing. He was taking deep breaths as he broke away and stared down at this wonderful woman in front of him that apparently wanted him as much as he wanted her.

Looking down at her, he couldn't help but smile at the sight of her swollen lips and flushed face. It was also nice to know she was just as out of breath as him.

"I've been waiting for that." Pulling her back to him for a quick hug, he released her and took a step back.

"I—I don't know what to say."

Before she could tuck her head down again, he grabbed her hand. "Say you want to go see some horses."

Nodding she squeezed his hand and led him towards the stables.

CHAPTER 5

"Tell me the truth, did you really enjoy petting the horses? You looked terrified." Tristan teased as they walked back into the bunk.

"I was scared, but I did like it." She was scared to death but made it through.

"Well, the stables aren't something we need photos of tomorrow, so you are off the hook from the horses for the rest of the trip." Winking he pulled her to him for a quick kiss.

The kiss, well kisses now, had been so unexpected she hadn't processed it still. All she had done was walk around in a happy daze with what she was sure was a stupid grin on her face. Couldn't make herself stop smiling, she tried.

"I should probably get dinner started; it looks like we have storms moving in."

"Dinner?"

"You didn't open the fridge at all?"

When she shook her head, he smiled and went to the fridge, pulling out 2 steaks, some salad, and a few other things.

"Oh my!"

"You get grilled steak for dinner tonight! Hope you're hungry."

"Famished. What can I help with?"

"You can get these on a plate to carry out and I will get the grill started." Opening the door and heading back outside, she had to admit, this was different than she had ever seen him.

That thought stuck with her as she unwrapped the steaks and got them onto a plate. He had a few seasonings set out, but she didn't know which ones or how much he wanted, so left it alone. Grabbing two beers from the fridge, she joined him out front.

"one for you." She set it next to the grill. "Do all the cabins have grills?"

"Bunks." He shot her a look. "And, yes."

"That's nice, so you can really get away from the city, no takeout or anything."

"You okay with it?"

"Yes! I mean I love it here, wish I had cell service though."

"It's one of the perks that's also a negative."

"I mean it's nice to be disconnected, but I feel bad, like I'm ignoring people." Grace took her lip in her mouth again and gently bit it, something she always did when she was worried. Truth was, she was ignoring two very specific someones, that hopefully weren't too worried about her.

"Tomorrow we will be looking at the conference center and there is signal there, we paid a lot for it, too."

"There's a conference center? What even is this place?"

Tristan through his head back and laughed. "It's part family friendly and part corporate team building. It was a way to bring in new customers and it has been very successful, but it needs a refresh to stay that way."

"That's awesome."

She was saved from having to come up with more conversation since he went to get the steaks. This had to be the longest she had held a conversation with Tristan in person. He hadn't run off at her attempts to talk and it had been mostly casual and easy. That stupid grin was creeping back up on her face, but she was feeling much better about it now.

Tristan came out and put both steaks on the grill. The conversation continued to flow. A little about work, a little about life in general. Neither of them brought up the kiss from earlier. Grace was dying to mention it and ask what it was about, but for now was trying to convince herself just to go with the flow, after all that had worked out for her so far, she ended up here.

A rumble of thunder interrupted her thoughts and before she could register what was happening, the sky had opened up on them and rain began to pour.

"Go on it, I will get these finished and join you." Tristan waved her away with his tongs.

"I will get the salad ready."

She had barely gotten the said put together as Tristan came in. He was soaked to the bone. His already fitted shirt now dripped as it clung to him, showing every muscle he had underneath.

"Some help you are." Tristan said, pulling her out of her daze.

"Oh my gosh, I'm so sorry." She ran and shut the door behind him.

"Don't apologize, I was just giving you a hard time."

"I—" Every thought in her head ran away as she spun around.

Tristan was in the middle of the room stripping out of his wet t-shirt. Everything she thought she had seen through the wet shirt was so much better out of it. Her tongue crept out and licked her lips without thought.

"Grace, I am trying so hard to keep myself under control here and be a gentleman, but I promise if you keep looking at me like that, I will not be able to hold on any longer."

She heard him, the growl in his voice. Saw the heat in his eyes, fiercer than it was before. She knew exactly what he meant, and it did nothing to make her want to stop looking at him, she was enjoying this trip more with each second.

A low growl came from him as he stalked across the room and crushed her mouth with his. She readily gave herself over to it. As she wrapped both arms around his neck, his hands dropped to her ass, lifting her up and pulling her towards him.

He pinned her there, in the air, pressed between him and the door in a kiss that could only be described as bone melting. She broke away and took a deep breath, but Tristan apparently didn't need to breath as he moved right down to her neck, kissing a trail from her ear to her shoulder.

"Tell me you want this too?" His voice was so low and gravely she didn't recognize it even as she nodded. "I want to hear it."

"I want this so much Tristan." She managed.

Tristan hesitated less than a second. "Hold on tight."

He pulled her away from the wall and carried her into his room. She couldn't help but giggle as she held on tight and buried her face into his shoulder. When they reached the bed, Tristan laid her down on the bed and climbed over her.

"This is not a laughing matter." He joked.

"I would have to agree with you there."

Tristan's mouth was on hers in the next instant. She didn't even have to think, her lips parted on their own as Tristan's tongue slid in as it had twice before today. The rush was gone from his kiss and it was lazier, exploratory, still just as hot.

"I have waited so long to kiss you like this." Tristan said as he broke the kiss and rested his forehead on hers.

Grace froze. Could it possibly be that he kept calling her because he wanted to see her as much as she wanted to see him? There was no way.

"I hate to rush things, and I mean that a lot, but I have to get these wet jeans off before we ruin the covers."

"Don't let me stop you." Grace copied his own move and raised an eyebrow at him.

"Oh, that's how it's going to be?" Tristan backed away from her and stood to remove his now plastered on jeans.

She was positive that had the jeans not been soaked through, he would have been the most graceful person she'd even seen. Instead the jeans required a lot of effort to get out of as they clung to him. She backed up onto the bed and propped herself on one elbow to watch him and tried to contain her laughter as he struggled.

"I thought we already discussed this not being a laughing matter?"

"That was something else entirely. This," she motioned up and down his legs, "is definitely a laughing matter."

Tristan stopped fighting with the jeans that were mostly off. "It seems to me that I am the only one that is getting undressed here." He pointed out.

Grace blushed. She sat up and struggled to find her confidence. She grabbed the bottom of her sweater and pulled it up over her head leaving only her bra behind.

"I had wondered."

"What?" Grace's eyes went wide with panic as she covered herself with her sweater.

"Don't do that." He climbed back onto the bed and laid her down as he removed the sweater and tossed it to the floor. "I have always wondered how far down your blush goes."

He trailed a finger from her cheek slowly down her chin, neck, and the valley between he breasts. "I have to know, is it under here too?" Looking up at her, she felt that he was again asking for her permission to move forward.

"I—I don't know."

"Let's find out?"

She nodded again, but this time he didn't wait for words as he slid his finger into her bra and lifted to take a look. Grace tossed her head back to the pillow, unable to think or use enough brain power to watch anything, just feel.

His hands came up to her shoulder and slid each bra strap down one at a time before freeing each breast and sucking in a breath. "I can't tell, better get a closer look."

She felt his breath on her nipple before his mouth. As soon as he took the first one into his mouth, she let out a small cry at the sheer pleasure of it as her eyes closed and she drank in the sensation.

"Hmm. Undetermined, maybe I should check the other." He didn't wait for a response as he lavished her other breast with the same attention he had with the other. His hand had cupped the other breast and was still providing it attention as his mouth worked.

Grace couldn't help herself as her tongue once again licked her lips of its own volition. Her kips moved below him, looking for the pleasure she knew he was offering.

"In the name of science, I think I should investigation just how far down you can blush." The words were lost on her as his hand left her breast and glided painfully slow down her stomach and into the waistband of her jeans.

She felt him use that one hand to undo the button and zipper of her jeans and slider into her panties. Her hips raised, seeking his hand, as he pulled his hand back out and backed up to help her out of her jeans.

The only thing she could think was *this is happening!* Over and over repeated in her brain until his finger slid deep inside her and all thought stopped. He slid his finger in and out as her hips began to match his rhythm. Meanwhile he slid his body back up hers and kissed her deeply again.

Adding a second finger, Tristan used his palm to give the pressure she needed to her center as their movements hurried looking for her pleasure. Breaking the kiss, she felt him lean back and his eyes on her face, watching as her pleasure grew.

With a tiny scream, Grace jumped over the edge and sank into a bright white bliss as she came into his hand. He slowed his movements as she rode the wave back down to Earth.

"That is single-handedly the best thing I have ever seen in my life." He kissed her again, sweetly and backed away. "Take those off."

She slid out of her panties and slipped her bra off as she watched Tristan find and roll on a condom. Her breathing was more and more rapid as she watched, ready for him to join her back on the bed.

Tristan looked at her in what could only be described as appreciation as he crawled onto the bed and up her body. "I want you so bad right now."

"I can't believe this is happening." Grace said as used his hands to move her legs apart.

In one swift move, Tristan was fully seated to the hilt within her. Grace gripped his arms as he began to move in her. She no longer cared what she looked like, what he was thinking, or what she should be thinking. Instead she closed her eye and enjoyed the sensations.

"You feel so good." Tristan moaned out.

Words brought her back to reality for a second, something she didn't want. She moved one hand to cover Tristan's mouth, "shut up."

He nipped at her fingers but didn't say anything else. Thunder rolled from outside again, threatening to pull her out of her bliss, she pushed it aside as the room got hotter and Tristan continued to pump.

Two hands went behind the back of her knees, pulling her legs further apart and up into the air. He was no longer hovering over her, instead he was straight upright, sweat on his brow as moans escaped them both.

Having never been loud during sex, one pump hit her in a spot that she hadn't known was there before and she arched up and cried out. He mumbled something to her and continued his assault on that spot until she yelled her release.

The room was spinning, stars were all she could see after a bright white light flashed and she started to slide down the other side of her peak, again. Tristan let out a guttural growl as he too reached his peak and stopped moving within her.

In the next moment, his sweaty body was collapsed on top of her own. It would have been a sweet gesture, always seemed like it in movies and in books, but Grace pushed his side to get him off of her.

"I can't breathe."

"Sorry." Tristan muttered and rolled over but didn't go far.

He wrapped one long arm over her and tucked her in next to him. They fit perfectly together and somehow, storm rolling outside, she slept.

CHAPTER 6

Tristan felt her breathing even out and knew Grace had fallen asleep. Reluctantly he rolled over and got out of bed. Never one to sleep immediately after sex, he put the room back to rights after tucking blankets around Grace.

Quietly he rummaged for some clothes is his suitcase and went to shower. This weekend was everything he wanted and more. Grace was amazing, and when she stopped being nervous around him, the conversations they had were amazing.

As he got out of the shower, he heard Grace walking past the door. "I'll be out in a moment." He yelled.

Quickly, he finished toweling off and opened the bathroom door to let her know she could have her turn. Instead he saw Grace wrapped in a sheet putting their forgotten dinner on plates in the kitchen.

"hungry?"

"A little." She blushed but didn't look at the floor, and Tristan gave a prayer of thanks that she was relaxed around him still. Not completely, but her loved her blushes.

"Well, let me help. Did you want to shower or eat first?"

Her stomach growled and they both laughed. "Eat, I think."

"I think so too."

He wrapped his arms around her waist as he approached her back in the kitchen. Nipping at her shoulder, he felt her shiver.

"Stop, you're going to make the sheet fall."

"My dear, that does nothing to deter me." He backed away anyway and walked to the fridge. "Beer or water?"

"Water, please."

Joining her at the table, he set two water bottles down. She had put the salad together on the plates and added each of them one of the steaks. She was putting dressing on her salad when she stopped and looked back at him.

"Is everything okay?"

Tristan nodded. Everything was great. He dug into his meal. The storm was still going outside, and the thunder rolled in the distance as they sat in quiet. It was a peaceful quiet, no stress, just enjoying their meals.

A short while later, Grace rose and carried her plate to the sink before announcing she was going to shower. Passing the time while she did, he cleaned up from their dinner and straightened the covers on his bed.

It was still early as far as things went. Pulling out a deck of cards, he hoped to talk her into playing a game with him when she came out. Instead as she stepped out of the bathroom, the scent of her hit him and his mouth went dry.

She was wearing shorts and a tank top, no bra, clearly just her usual sleepwear, but her hair was still wet, resting on her shoulders. She looked refreshed and he just wanted to take her again, breathe in her peachy scent. He may have to snoop and see what she used that smelled so good.

"Cards?" She asked him.

Tristan cleared his throat, "Yeah."

"Let me brush my hair and I'm game. What are we playing?"

They discussed a few different games as she did her hair in the bathroom mirror. It was such an intimate feeling to be having a causal conversation as she brushed out her hair, cutting a look at him every now and then.

In the end, they settled on a game of Rummy and established the rules. She beat him in 4 games before she started yawning. It wasn't until she did that, he considered he had no idea what their sleeping arrangements would be after earlier. He certainly hoped she wanted to sleep with him, it was definitely what he wanted.

Tristan put away the deck of cards and held his hand up to help her out of the chair, only a little disappointed that she wasn't still wearing the sheet that could slide off at any time.

"Ready for bed?" he asked.

"I think so." Grace followed that with another yawn and a laugh.

"Sleep with me?" He watched her reaction to see if she really wanted to.

She shook her head and his heart dropped to his toes. "No, you sleep with me, my bed's clean."

All his breath came out in a whoosh as relief hit him. "Fair point." He said as he led her into the bedroom. He turned down the covers and waited for her to climb in before climbing in and curling up to her.

Her sigh as she wiggled closer to him was all her need to content himself into a comfortable sleep. He rarely slept long, or well, hazards of a stressful job, but tonight he knew it was going to be the best night's sleep he'd had in a while.

* * *

THE NEXT MORNING Tristan reached out to find an empty bed beside him. No warmth left; she must have been up for a while he thought. Stretching, he tossed back the covers and stood to go looking for her.

The bunk was completely empty, she was nowhere to be found except for a pot of coffee showing she had been here this morning. Tristan poured himself a cup and went to the porch in search of Grace.

Not hard to find, she had gotten dressed and was outside with her camera, completely oblivious to him. He stood there for a bit and watched her, fully immersed in her work with a smile on her face, snapping a few photos and then checking the screen to see how they looked.

"Good morning!" He yelled, snapping her out of her trance.

"Good morning! I see you found the coffee." Joining him on the porch, she surprised him by going up on her tiptoes for a kiss.

He raised his empty hand and ran it through her long brown hair. "I did, thank you." Smiling she stepped back. "What are you taking pictures of?"

"A little of everything. I don't get a chance to be in different settings often, thought I would take advantage of it."

"Can I see?"

Blushing again, she nodded. "Let me pull them up on the computer and you can take a look before we get started with today's works."

He sipped his coffee and waited as she opened her laptop and slid in a memory card. Standing over her shoulder at the table, he watched as she clicked through the photos she had taken. He knew she was good, but he was impressed with the photos from today.

"It's amazing the angles and lighting, the way you know how to get the best photos." He wasn't exaggerating. "We should have you come back when guests are here and get some shots of the ranch for the website."

"Oh, I'd love that!" Turning her full smile on him, he felt a thrill rush through him.

"It's a date!" he said and walked away before she had a chance to say anything else.

He got dressed and they toured the buildings he did need photos of while Grace did her usual of following behind him and making small noises to assure him, she was listening. She snapped photos as she went, and when the tour was over, he pulled out his laptop to check on a few things at work and lost track of Grace.

This was normal for them whenever he hired her for a job. She always went off into her own thing and then caught up with him when she was done. With anyone before he, he usually just left and then got emails later with the photos, with Grace, he always waited.

Something about the photos she took worked magic for his own creative mind. She seemed to understand exactly what he needed, and the results were amazing. He had told her once before and meant it, she was his muse. Her photos were exactly what he needed to get his creative juices flowing and as part owner of this ranch, he wanted to put his best work into the renovations more than ever before.

He had also been serious earlier this morning, she was hired to help take photos of the ranch in full swing. She could help him revamp the website. Clicking through the current website he realized some of the pictures had to have been more than a decade old.

Tristan opened a new file on his tablet and started taking notes on the changes he wanted to see to the website and where Grace could help. He was so lost in what he was doing, he nearly dropped his table when she came up.

"I think I have what I need." She said and immediately started laughing. "I didn't know I could scare you; I believe that redeems my pride for having been so jumpy yesterday."

He smiled at her and gave her a kiss on the forehead. "You want to work here or go back to the bunk?"

She looked around and then took in everything he had spread out in front of him. "I think we would outgrow the bunk rather quickly if we both tried to work in it."

Grace sat down on the other end of the long table he was already at and opened her own laptop. He was happy she was content to work there next to him but also in her own space. He'd had women that wanted to constantly stand over his shoulder and he couldn't get anything done.

His last relationship had ended over a year ago and at the time he had thrown himself even more into the firm, if that was even possible. He already worked too much but was hoping to make the ranch more profitable for his uncle and be able to work less for the firm in person.

He would love to move up this way and work more remotely and a lot less. He had grown up here on the ranch with his uncle after his parents had passed away. This was home for him, and he was ready to come back.

When he was done with his notes, he looked down to find Grace with her head buried into her laptop. Packing up his stuff took a bit of time but the next time he looked up, Grace was smiling back at him.

"Come see." She waved him over.

He rarely got to see her work as she did it for him. She normally left and went home to work on them. Anything he saw was on the camera itself as she confirmed that she had gotten what he wanted. Now, he was thrilled to see what she had gotten.

"I got the usual standard shots that I will send over, but here are my photos of the buildings."

She slid over and he took the seat in front of the computer and began to slide through the photos. There were no words to see what she had captured of the place he grew up. The building they were in was an old barn, that in his childhood had served as a gathering place before the lodge building was set up.

She had managed to get the character of the inside and the outside of this building and the two next door. Something that only she managed to understand, the history here, shots of the old doors, things that she somehow knew he would incorporate into the renovation.

These photos would help him tremendously as he worked on designing the renovations. He knew what he wanted to keep, and she had gotten everything. Now he could take those photos and put them into his design and start work soon.

"This is wonderful." Turning to her, he put an arm around her. "As always."

Grace dropped her head on his shoulder. "I'm glad. Are you going to keep most of the old features?"

"You never ask about the plans." He pointed out.

"I didn't mean to overstep." Lifting her head, he realized he had definitely put his foot in his mouth.

"No, stay, I didn't mean anything bad. I want to share this with you. I hope you'll be around to see the work get completed with me?"

"I hope so too," came her small reply.

Tristan launched into what he had envisioned for the changes to this building. She made a few comments here and there, things that he hadn't noticed about details of the building. Occasionally she snapped a few photos as he walked through the rooms with her.

"I think this is going to look amazing. I can't wait to see it."

Tristan felt his chest fill with pride. He knew with her by his side, this was going to be his best project yet.

78

ALSO BY TONI DENISE

Learn More at tonidenisebooks.com

Westbeach Series:

Old Friends

On the Run

One Last Chance

Out of Time

Finding Love Series

Engaged to Her Neighbor

Married to the Playboy

Falling for Her Fake Husband

Short and Steamy Duet

The Wedding Date

The Wedding Ruse

Stone Twins Duet:

Please Stay

Don't Leave

(Don't Leave is included in the "Mine This Winter" collection
available Dec 1, 2022)

Billionaire Blind Dates:

Jake

KEEP IN TOUCH!

Follow Toni Denise on Social Media!
Facebook
Instagram
Twitter

And Sign up for her Newsletter to find out about awesome
games and new releases.
Sign up here!

ENGAGED TO HER NEIGHBOR
SNEAK PEEK

Macy is starting over in a new town with her little brother to take care of. She settled on a small town where no one knows their past and they can be themselves without the shadow their father casts over them.

Daniel agreed to rent his property, but it was supposed to be simple instead, a kid and a dog interrupt his life from day one. Annoyed by the disturbance, he pushes them away until the day he really needs them.

When Daniel gets injured and Macy comes to the rescue, feelings get in the way. Macy agrees to help Daniel until he's recovered but never could have predicted that the arrival of Daniel's ex-fiance would lead to a fake engagement for herself.

Sparks fly when the town gets involved in the fake wedding and Macy and Daniel have to decide what they really want from each other. How far will they take this fake engagement? Can it become real?

Turn the page for a sneak peek of Chapter One!

ENGAGED TO HER NEIGHBOR
CHAPTER ONE

What is going on? There was a kid in his yard, and a dog too. Daniel headed off his porch to investigate, leaning heavily on his cane. Today was not a good pain day and the last thing he needed to be doing was trekking across the yard in search of answers as to who the wayward dog and child belonged to.

He stopped and rubbed his knee as he made it to the bottom of the steps wincing as the pain shot up his leg before calming back down to its normal dull ache. The worst part was over until it was time to go back inside, stairs made the pain worse, walking more than just around his house was a close second to it.

The dog noticed him before the kid did and stopped chasing the ball and ran straight for Daniel. He braced for impact, but the dog stopped before reaching him and sniffed at him. He took in the yellow, almost white, dog before him. It was gentle, just inquisitive, sniffing him as though sizing him up as well. Daniel stuck his hand out for the dog to sniff and when he felt like he had received approval he patted the dog on the head that was almost reaching his waist and waited for the boy to approach.

* * *

At least it wasn't raining, that was the only positive part of the day so far. Macy and her brother were supposed to be moving into the new house she had rented them today and everything that could go wrong so far, had. It was more stress than one person should have to deal with.

It all started when she tried to start the rented truck with all their belongings in it, of course the battery was dead. Skipping the costs on roadside assistance had seemed an easy way to save a few bucks, but it just figured she'd need it. Sixty bucks later she had paid someone to come out and jump the battery from the local tow company, and the rest of the day had been much the same. They got a late start, then she had to stop and get food for her and Chris because they had left the peanut butter and jelly sandwiches, that she had packed for them in her car, which of course was at the rental truck place.

The two-hour drive to their new home had been filled with traffic and two complete stops, taking them more than double what it should have. They were so far behind and now she needed to get everything out of the truck so she could return it tomorrow and get her car. She had only taken two days off for this move mentally and needed to get to finding a new job right away, plus she didn't want to pay for an extra day for the rental truck either.

Finally getting to the house which she had rented based off pictures online, she realized there was no way she was going to be able to back the truck down this long, narrow driveway, so now they were adding extra steps to everything. Now Chris had disappeared under the guise of taking Lucy, their lab, for a walk, leaving her to do it all on her own. Chasing him down would waste more time and honestly, he wasn't that much help, one trip to her three, but it was one less thing she had to carry at least.

Sighing, she set down the boxes she had carried in and went in search of Chris and Lucy. Yelling for him, she went through the small one-story house in search of them with no luck. Heading through the back door, she looked out into the yard for them, not seeing them anywhere. She yelled for them and heard Lucy bark, but no one came running. Deciding there was no hope for it, she stepped off the small back porch and went in the direction of the sound.

Looking around, she noticed that the pictures she had seen had done very little justice to the outdoor space here. There was just one neighbor, whose house she could just barely see from hers as it was a good walk away and sat higher than hers on a hill. It was that beautiful green hill that she climbed now. Whoever live here definitely took care of their yard because this was the greenest grass she had ever seen. It took considerable restraint on her part not to take off her shoes and see how it felt under her bare feet.

Smiling and slightly winded, she reached the top of the hill and looked upon a gorgeous two-story house made out of wood. This would be a perfect example of one of those log cabins from the shows on TV where people spend an insane amount of money building a vacation home that they intend to use only a few times a year.

Looking around she spotted Chris and Lucy with a man standing near the woods at the back of their properties. Macy cringed, as she knew how Chris felt about men with the way that their father had treated them. The boy was only eight and should have been running around without a care in the world, instead he was standing there head down, shuffling his feet and listening to the man talk. Lucy noticed her and came running over to greet her and walked with her to Chris.

I hope he hasn't made the new neighbors mad already. I hope that man isn't yelling at him either. Her head swirled with thoughts as she approached them.

The man was dressed in jeans and a solid grey t-shirt and was leaning on a cane with his left hand. He needed a haircut she noticed as she walked closer, it was past the point of touching his ears, but not long enough to be considered long hair. He had a full scruffy beard to match his brown hair that he was reaching up to scratch as she walked up. He looked like an untamed mountain man, one that definitely preferred to be left alone. The look he was giving her now definitely said that he didn't welcome distractions, especially in the form of a rambunctious dog and small boy.

"Hi, I'm Macy, we are moving in next door." She stuck out her hand to greet the man.

"Daniel, and I had guessed as much." He shook her hand. "I hope not to find everyone wandering around in my back yard now that you live here."

"No sir, I will make sure they know where the property line is." She put her hand on Chris's shoulder. "I'm sorry I was unloading the truck and I lost track of them."

The man looked at her. It was more than a look, it was a hard stare, taking her measure and clearly judging her parenting skills, finding them lacking. "See to it that you keep a better eye on them in the future."

With that the man turned and limped away, leaning heavily on his cane. She turned to Chris to fuss at him, but he still had his head down, clearly bothered by running into Daniel on his first day here.

"I'm sorry Macy, I didn't know I wasn't supposed to go this far."

"It's okay bud, you do now. If you had been helping though I would have been able to tell you after we got the truck unloaded."

Chris nodded and then headed down the hill towards their little house. Macy had decided it was in the best interest for both of them to move farther away from their hometown to get away from their father. He was in jail now for hitting a woman while he was driving drunk and injuring her pretty badly. She had lived, but barely. Even though he was locked up and they had nothing to do with it, the stigma of being Joe Manning's kids had followed them around before and had only gotten worse after the accident.

They had been treated as trash their whole lives simply because of parentage and their father hadn't treated them much better. She hadn't called him Dad in so long she had forgotten the last time she had. He wasn't a Dad; Joe was a drunk, and a mean one at that.

Macy's mom had passed away when she was too young to remember her well, then Joe had raised her, if you could call it that. She just remembered being alone all the time, and the endless string of neighbors that used to help watch her until Joe did something to make them stop watching her too. They moved around from trailer park to trailer park, sometimes only staying on someone else's couch because Joe never would hold down a job long.

Then Joe met Candice, or Candy as she was known to everyone else. How they managed to live together for nearly a year was something she never understood. Candy hadn't stuck around long after Chris was born, and then had just disappeared one day. From then on it had been Macy that took care of Chris.

She was only fifteen when he was born, it had made her scared to leave him with Joe while she went to school. Then she had come across an older neighbor that kept Chris for her while she was in school in exchange for Macy cleaning her house and helping her cook meals whenever she could.

It wasn't until she was a few years older and Ms. Mary

had passed away that she realized Mary had just been protecting them and teaching Macy all the things that a mom would have taught her. She was their safe harbor in the storm that was their lives and Macy had cried like she had never done before when Ms. Mary had passed away. Joe had refused to take them to the funeral, which had also hurt.

She would have moved out then and tried to make her own way in the world instead of paying bills for Joe, but she couldn't do that to Chris. She had done her absolute best to keep him as sheltered from their father's violent tirades as she could, taking the brunt of his anger, but if she wasn't there anymore, it would all be at Chris.

Shortly after she turned 21, a lawyer contacted her; apparently Mary had a will and had put Macy in it. She had left her a nice sum of money but had decided that she couldn't know of it, or come into it until she was legally old enough to not have to give any to Joe. Ten thousand dollars was a lot of money then and Macy had thought hard about what to do with it.

It had been two years now and she was just reaching out to use it, starting with getting custody of Chris as soon as Joe's trial was over. Then they rented this house, paying for the deposit and a few months rent all at once. It gave her time to get settled into her new job before the big bill of rent was due, which was considerably more than they had been paying at the trailer. They would make it work though; she was sure of it.

They worked until past dark to get the truck unloaded and didn't have time to set anything up. Instead she and Chris curled up on their mattresses on the floor in sleeping bags once everything was in the house. She had found the small cooler with the sandwiches she had made yesterday for today's lunch in the back of the truck, making it so she didn't have to spend more money on food for the night.

She looked over at Chris, curled up with Lucy on his bed, hugging her protectively. She had been the one thing that made Chris feel safe, and she had always done her best to live up to that feeling. Lucy had bitten Joe once on his hand, he had cussed up a storm, but that was the last time he had ever attempted to hit Chris again, for which Macy had been grateful and rewarded Lucy with dinner scraps ever since, she had earned her place in their family.

Macy rolled onto her back and stared up at the ceiling, thinking about this decision. She hoped she could find a job and a sitter within the next two weeks or they were screwed. This plan had been thought out as intensely as she could with the exception of a job, she couldn't make the drive out here for interviews ahead of time, so she prayed that she would find one when Chris started school on Wednesday. With luck it would pay enough for her to only need to work during the day and not require her to get a sitter for after school.

Sleep wouldn't come and after laying there and worrying for too long, she got up and grabbed her cell phone before laying back down. Lucy had lifted her head to watch her but hadn't left Chris's side. Unlocking her phone, she started scrolling through the job postings for Allensville, VA.